GUMDROP
Catches a Cold

Gumdrop is a <u>real</u> car owned by artist and author Val Biro. Horace is his <u>real</u> dog.

In this story Gumdrop gets very ill.

You will read some new words in this book:

crank	hospital
engine	mechanic
garage	oil cans
gas station	pumped
grease guns	tuned up
hammers	wrenches
hood	

You can look up what they mean and how to use them on pages 4 and 5.

Library of Congress Cataloging-in-Publication Data

Biro, Val, date.
    Gumdrop catches a cold.

    (Gumdrop quickstart readers)
    Includes index.
    Summary: When Gumdrop, a vintage car, catches a cold, his
owner is concerned by his sneezing and wheezing and must save
him from falling apart.
    (1. Automobiles–Fiction.   2. Cold (Disease)–Fiction.   3. Sick–
Fiction) I. Title. II. Series.
PZ7.B5233Gtdm 1985   (E)   85-12689
ISBN O-918831-14-8 (lib. bdg.)
ISBN O-918831-58-X (trade bdg.)

ISBN O-918831-14-8 lib. bdg.
ISBN O-918831-58-X trade bdg.

North American edition first published in 1985 by

Gareth Stevens, Inc.
7221 W. Green Tree Road
Milwaukee, WI 53223

First published in the United Kingdom by Hodder & Stoughton
Children's Books with an original text copyright by Val Biro.

Typeset by Colony Pre-Press • Milwaukee, WI 53208

Reading Consultant: Libby Gifford
Designer: Sharon Burris

GUMDROP
Catches a Cold

Story and Pictures by Val Biro

Gareth Stevens–Milwaukee

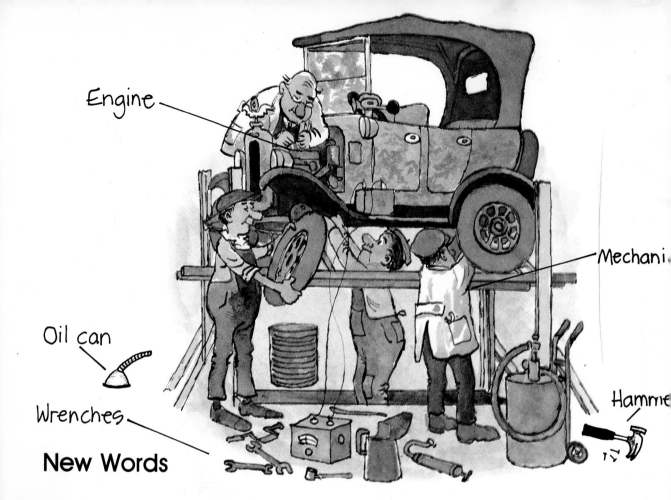

Engine

Mechani

Oil can

Wrenches

Hammer

New Words

Crank	a handle used to start an older car. I turned the <u>crank</u> to start the car.
Engine	the part of the car that makes it go. The car <u>engine</u> ran well.
Garage	a place where cars are fixed. I took my car to the <u>garage</u> to get it fixed.
Gas station	a place to buy gas. I buy gas at the <u>gas station</u>.
Grease guns	tools that shoot grease into parts of a car. We used <u>grease guns</u> to fix the squeaky wheels.
Hammers	tools used to hit things into place. We used <u>hammers</u> to hit the nails into the wood

4

Hood

the part of the car that covers the engine.
I closed the <u>hood</u> after I put oil into the engine.

Hospital

a place where people go to get well.
I went to the <u>hospital</u> to get well.

Mechanic

a person who fixes cars.
The <u>mechanic</u> fixed Joe's car.

Oil cans

cans that squirt oil into car engines.
The <u>oil cans</u> spilled and made the floor slippery.

Pumped

filled with air.
We <u>pumped</u> up the tires when they got flat.

Tuned up

made a car engine run at its best.
The mechanic <u>tuned up</u> the car's engine.

Wrenches

tools used for turning nuts and bolts.
(Nuts and bolts hold parts of a car together.)
Joe uses <u>wrenches</u> to take the wheels off.

5

The morning was sunny. Joe walked over to Gumdrop. Gumdrop is Joe's car.

"What a good day for a drive," said Joe. "Let's go, Gumdrop!" Joe turned the crank, but Gumdrop did not start. Joe tried again. Still no luck!

8

Joe called his friends. "Gumdrop needs some help. Give us a push, please," he said.

So Joe's friends pushed and pushed. Gumdrop tried hard to start. Joe's friends pushed even harder.

Bang! Suddenly Gumdrop started. Joe's friends jumped. "Thanks!" Joe called. Joe and Gumdrop drove away. Gumdrop started to squeak.

Soon the sky grew dark. The rain came fast. Inside and out poor old Gumdrop got soaking wet. The squeaking got louder and louder.

Then Gumdrop started to hiss and wheeze. "You are not very well," said Joe. He pressed Gumdrop's horn. "A-tchooo! A-tchooo!" went the horn. "Oh dear!" said Joe. "It sounds like you have a cold!"

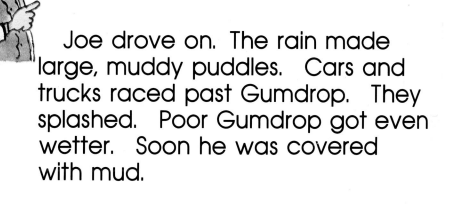

Joe drove on. The rain made large, muddy puddles. Cars and trucks raced past Gumdrop. They splashed. Poor Gumdrop got even wetter. Soon he was covered with mud.

Joe drove Gumdrop to a gas station. Gumdrop stopped with a clatter. A mechanic looked at Gumdrop. "That car needs help," he said. "The engine is in a real mess. It is too hot. Feel the hood!"

Joe felt Gumdrop's hood. "Gumdrop has caught a cold," said Joe. The mechanic gave Joe a funny look.

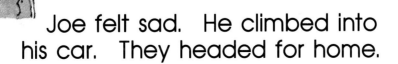

Joe felt sad. He climbed into his car. They headed for home.

Suddenly, Gumdrop began to bump and jerk. Other drivers waved their arms. They pointed at the front wheel. Soon a driver called to Joe, "Your car has a flat tire!"

Joe stopped. He got out of Gumdrop. Yes, a front tire was flat. Just then a friend drove up. Her two girls called to Joe, "Your old car is full of spots! Gumdrop should see a doctor."

Luckily there was a garage close by. It was called "The Car Hospital."

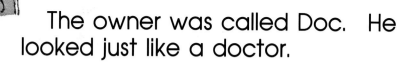

The owner was called Doc. He looked just like a doctor.

Doc lifted the hood. He looked at the engine. He turned on the engine. He tapped and he poked. He listened and said, "Aha!" and "Hmm!"

Doc stood up and smiled. "Give us just one day, Joe. We'll make Gumdrop well."

22

Joe covered Gumdrop with a blanket. He patted his car on the hood. "Don't worry, old friend," said Joe. "I'll be back. You'll get well."

Doc and the other mechanics went to work, with hammers and wrenches, with grease guns and oil cans and a bunch of other tools.

They tuned up Gumdrop's engine. They pumped up the tire. They gave the old car a warm bath. Then they put Gumdrop back on the floor.

Joe came back in the morning. Gumdrop looked as good as new. He got in and turned the key. Gumdrop started on the first try. Joe smiled. Gumdrop sounded good.

Then Joe paid Doc, thanked him and drove off. Doc waved a happy goodbye.

Index of New Words

Gumdrop and the Farmyard Caper

Gumdrop, Joe, and Horace go camping. Horace is Joe's pet puppy. What happens when Horace chases all the farm animals and meets a hungry fox?

Gumdrop Floats Away

Gumdrop, Joe, and Horace go fishing. Joe and Horace fall asleep. And Gumdrop floats away at high tide - with Horace on board! Can Joe save them?

Gumdrop and the Great Sausage Caper

Horace finds some sausage, and then gets chased by an angry crowd of people and a mean bulldog. Can Horace escape? And what do Joe and Gumdrop do?

31

Gumdrop Is the Best

Joe's friends think Gumdrop is no good. "Buy a new car!" they tell Joe. "Buy one just like mine!" Are those other cars really better than Gumdrop?

Gumdrop at the Zoo

A camel gets sick - so no camel rides for the children today. Can Gumdrop save the day? Fun and games at the zoo with Joe and his grandson, Dan. And, of course, with Gumdrop, the famous vintage car.

Ask for these books about Gumdrop, your favorite vintage car.